To Kimmi, Ari, Milo, Mom, Dad, Rebecca,
Josh, Gracie, Farfel, and all fun dogs!
—E.T.B.

For my dogs, Rosie and George,
who will probably never read this
—J.C.

Visit us on the Web! rhcbooks.com

Educators and librarians, for a variety of teaching tools, visit us at RHTeachersLibrarians.com

Library of Congress Cataloging-in-Publication Data
Names: Berlin, Ethan T., author. | Chapman, Jared, illustrator.
Title: I am not a dog toy / by Ethan T. Berlin ; illustrated by Jared Chapman.
Description: First edition. | New York : Random House Children's Books, [2021] | Audience: Ages 3–7. | Audience: Grades K–1. |
Summary: "A stuffed bear looking for a best friend believes he is meant to be a child's toy,
but true friendship comes to him from a place he least expects." —Provided by publisher.
Identifiers: LCCN 2019051697 (print) | LCCN 2019051698 (ebook)
ISBN 978-0-593-11901-3 (hardcover) | ISBN 978-0-593-11902-0 (library binding) | ISBN 978-0-593-11903-7 (ebook)
Subjects: CYAC: Teddy bears—Fiction. | Dogs—Fiction. | Humorous stories.
Classification: LCC PZ7.1.B458 Iam 2021 (print) | LCC PZ7.1.B458 (ebook) | DDC [E]—dc23

The artist set up his studio in a kennel to create the illustrations.
Book design by Nicole de las Heras
MANUFACTURED IN CHINA
10 9 8 7 6 5 4 3 2 1
First Edition

I AM NOT A DOG TOY

written by
Ethan T. Berlin

illustrated by
Jared Chapman

Random House 🏠 New York

HELLO!
I'm going to be your most
favorite toy ever!

But I'll play with you
all the time! I will love you!
And chew you! And lick you!
And chew you!

That is such a unique offer.
But I am not a dog toy.

Dog toys are torn-up,
disgusting things that
weren't good enough
to be kids' toys.

And I am a fancy kids' toy
with lots of pockets.

You have so
many pockets!

Thank you!

Also, you are a dog toy.
Because I'm a dog and we're
going to play together!

Wasn't that the most fun ever?
You're totally a dog toy!

First, that was not the most fun ever!
Second, that was so much fun!
And third, I am not a dog toy!

See, here comes my best friend, a kid, to rescue me from you, a dog.

What is this thing doing on my bed?!

Um, I don't think she is your friend.
She threw you into the wedge.

Only toys she doesn't like
go into the wedge.

I AM A KIDS' TOY!

And this kid
is going to play with me!

Maybe you should consider playing
with a really fun dog.

No, no, no!
I'm supposed to be a kids' toy!

I'm going to find someone who wants to be my best friend. Someone who likes to fight bad guys and build forts and fight different bad guys!

Someone who thinks it's really cool that I have so many pockets!

Someone who is fun to play with and would never put me in the wedge.

Let's run around in circles!